Spitt-16 Book's

Presents

"Taijae's Illusion"

La'mar Donald

LLC.

Taijae's Illusion©2021 By La'mar Donald

Artwork by CHOPPTRIGG@Element Of Design

First edition

All characters, events and organizations produced in this novel is a work of fiction, a product of the writers imagination. Any similarities in characters, names and places are coincidental.

This book is dedicate Dirty Di. My lil Gunshine...

La'mar Donald

Taijae's illusion

Taijae Taylor lived a plain yet simple life upon until she met Tanacia Thompson, a dear friend and associate who seems to always be caught up in the mix and on a girls day out they coincedently find Artencie Fulton, one of Tanacia's co-workers dead in a wooded area near the plaza. The same plaza where Tanacia is getting a fill-in.

"Question is who committed these murder and their motive, what is it that they are trying to hid or just maybe people with power like proving a point."

You decide.

Part 1

The people always said that my friend Tanacia Thompson was a fashion guru. Her closet consists of nothing but designer gear and its funny because she never wore the same hairstyle two days straight and the chick at the nail salon had to be well payed much as she stayed with a fill in.

But unlike most people I took the time and got better acquainted with her.

She was sensible and down to earth but she clearly had problems and some how or another she was always in the wrong place at the wrong time.

What I like to call "problematic," but the sweetest little thing you could ever meet but always in a jam and if you hung around Tenacia long enough you to would end up in the crossfire too.

"It was kind of like a cold, really contagious. Take it from me, I experienced it first hand."

 I'm far from a saint and you can trust that I've had my share of the bull with plenty to come.

As for me, my name is Taijae Taylor and I started the H.P.F.O. The High Performance Female Organization and I wouldn't doubt that you've seen my sisters and I on our local news a time or too.

During the holidays we donated to the needy families then there's been more than one incident where I helped someone who was being assaulted.

 Somehow someone recorded me in action this last time and it went viral, causing people to looked at me from a different angle.

 Treated me like I was Queen Njinga giving me a

tad bit tyo much of recognition. In H.P.F.O. there was about hundred women or so but Mazzy, Kelley Renée and V'naevia Swift were my ace coonboon's and they too had gained a little recognition which with time slowly faded away.

That's just the way it was. To most we were just another group of Afrian american females from the hood with good office jobs.

Truth is we are just your average everyday, I mean take me for starters. I've been labeled simple and plain and my ex husband once told me I was "par for the course."

 I later learned what that really meant.

At the age of thirty-six I couldn't complain.

You know the saying, but when life handed me lemons I chased it with vodka.

"The eldest of the women in my group was a sixty year old retired Marine navigational specialist, that was Mazzy.

 Then there's V'naevia Swift who just recently opened up a traveling agency with no kind of flavor when it came to men."

"This I knew because she was my best friend, and how could I forget about Kelley Renée the life of P.F.O. For one she was young and foxy, sagacious as they say and green with envy."

"Personally I'm still trying to find myself and the feeling of being unimportant is eating away at me like cancer."

"My ex husband Edris always reminded me that I was to helpful and how it would one day come back to haunt me and the day I encountered Tanacia adversities was the day she treated me and Danja on a girls day out."

"Adversities!" I wonder if that's the proper way to word the episodes that occurred in Tanacia's little world?

Personally I need your opinion. This is just how it went down.

"Danja!," Tanacia shrieked as soon as she set foot in my luxurious crash pad.

 For a moment she acted as if i didn't exist as she waltzed past me in the direction of my living room dropping her Mui Mui clutch purse embracing my eighty pound guardian angel.

Danja turned a few circle as if she were chasing her tail before she laid out flat on her back for Tanacia to rub her belly. I guess she was glad to see Tanacia too.

"Danja," Girl looks like you've put on a few pounds and today we shall shed a few, I hope your ready for some fun, replied Tanacia.

"Danja might be but I truely don't feel up to it," I replied from the kitchen as I grabbed a bottled water from the fridge.

Soon as I set foot in the living room Danja gave me that look. The same look of excitement she had when Pit bulls and parolees or Garfield the cat was on television.

I had adopted her and her brother when they were six weeks old, seconds from being euthanized. Danja was what they called a bully, she was jet black like a panther with gray eyes, the bias of a human being and a head to big to fit in a five gallon bucket and this year made seven years that we'd been in cahoots and I can't and want lie. Hands down she was the best friend and pet a girl could have.

"I can honestly say that she's held me down like balloon strings."

Finally Tanacia got to her feet and gave me a hug and said," I have the whole day to planned perfection. First we are going to stop by the nail shop. Then Danja is going to visit my friend Retro Active at Pitbull passion kennels for a much needed make over and we my friend are dining at Cajun Asia's, for some odd reason I got a taste for curry fried shrimp, hush puppies and some of Asia's special sauce.

The tips of Danja's clipped ears twitched as she wobbled over to Tanacia wagging her tail joyfully like she knew and understood everything that was taking place.

Tanacia said, "How about Daric Darnell let me borrow the Porsche Cayenne, my poor little bucket is in the shop and I've got to have this thing back before seven so how about we tighten up, time is rolling and it ain't like we go all day."

I looked at my watch and it was ten minutes to twelve and partially cloudy on this second Saturday in September.

The sun peeked out occasionally from behind the thick gray clouds that had built up causing the air to feel thick and dense.

"Hold a second," I replied as I ran back inside to get an umbrella.

Tanacia looked up at the sky and said, "Don't worry, I'm almost one hundred percent positive that it'll blow over, rain or not we're going to enjoy this and just imagine, people in hell are definitely drinking ice water cause you know Daric Darnell would never let a soul drive his cars and this opportunity happens once in a life time plus I promised Danja that I would take her out and there isn't anyway I'm not going to enjoy this plus I planned this week's ago and ain't going for nothing strange."

Outside sitting in my drive way was a ghost white Porsche suv,

Tanacia opened the door and Danja hopped right in.

Tanacia gave me a tiresome look and said, "Honestly I don't feel like dealing with this traffic and I would love for you to handle my light weight but if something happened to Daric's whip, I wouldn't hear the end of it and I sure as hell came pay for it."

Daric Darnell was Tanacia's boss, what many considered to be a head honcho and if you had a problem big or small he was the man to call.

He was some what important with a lot of power along with majority of the people he were friends with.

Darnell and associates was a family owned law firm that won cases. Civil, federal you name it. Four years ago he hired Tanacia as his secretary and it wasn't a surprise that her credentials landed her the role of his personal accountant.

Tanacia pushed the start button and the SUV came to life, we strapped our seat belts and the next thing I knew we were in rotation with traffic.

As we drove down the express way I couldn't help but look up at the sky thru the panoramic roof which made the sky appear gloomier than it really was.

I then looked over at Tanacia who had more flavor than a box of fruit loops.

She wore a stripped Polo shirt, gray and pink in color, a denim mini skirt along with a matching pair of ninety five Airmax's.

I also noticed that she wore little to no make up and the nail on her right index finger was broken.

I on the other hand wore my usual, a pair of Level 99 jeans, a purple novelty tee that read "Keep that same energy," and a pair of purple and black hurraches.

Dressing up was something I hardly ever done and to clear up the rumors that you may have heard, it is true what they say, I am well off.

My aunt down in Miami died about three years ago and left stocks in Black rocks along with sixty-eight acres of beach front properties.

Unknowingly I inherited everything she owned due to the fact that she never had kids.

As we cruised along Halsey's hit single "Devil in me" blared through the factory speakers of the SUV then out of nowhere Tanacia said, "I wish Ms.Fulton could see a bitch now, she would be madder than five hundred hell and probably want to kill me if she knew I even look in the direction of this vehicles."

"I have no I idea what the two of them have going

on and personally I don't care but for some reason she thinks she runs shit. Yesterday she scolded me about my tounge ring saying it was unprofessional."

"I told her to stop looking in my mouth, Daric just happen to be walking by and jump down her throat for complaining about every little thing. I know for a fact they've had flings and she is the jealous type."

"She see's how Daric

looks at me and I do to but I don't entertain none of that plus he's like fifty-ish, old enough to be my daddy."

"That old school dumpster been getting trash."

As Tanacia drove and talked, I listened.

 She said, "Yesterday on my way out of the office I heard Daric tell Ms.Fulton to "Fix it before someone gets hurt."

I asked, "What do you think that meant?"

Tanacia said, "Now what she is suppose to fix, I have no idea but I know this man and he was dead serious."

Tanacia grew silent as she starred off in traffic then said, "It's no secret, I know she doesn't like me, you should see how she looks at me. Looks that would kill."

"She tells me I cant, Daric tells me I can."

****

Artencie Fulton had been with the firm for about twelve years and was Daric's executive assistant from day one.

"She was aware and knew about everything that went on behind those walls but my question was why was she so mad with Tanacia."

Tanacia said, "She hates me with a passion, its written all over her face."

I had be logic about this. For starters Artencie Fulton was Daric's number one and I'm pretty sure that came with a lot of pressure not including the four other attorneys that worked the firm not to mention the computer and paper work that she kept up with," I replied as I looked down at Tanacia's hundred and fifty dollar tennis shoes.

"Tanacia was ten years younger than I was but

that didn't make a difference, at the time when we met she needed me and friends didn't let friends drive drunk did they!"

We turned off the express way and the traffic had lightened up just a little and so did the sky.

In the very back of the SUV Danja paced from one side to another excitedly as we pulled into the parking lot of the plaza where the nail shop was located.

On the far east end of the plaza was a small park with grills, picnic tables and just enough space for Danja to stretch.

While we waited for Tanacia to get that one nail repaired, I sat at a wooden picnic table and watched as Danja covered every square inch of the park.

The dark clouds hid the sun broadcasting a devastatingly gloomy yet depressing lunch hour.

My call phone vibrated twice interfering with my thoughts.

I glanced at the screen, it was one of my tenant's in Miami who had been nagging about buying some property that I had no intention of selling.

He'd offered me a few million a week before and today he added another eighty to that.

Once again I declined, "No deal jack!"

Time was rolling because before I knew it Tanacia had returned breaking me out my trance.

She said, "Where is Danja?"

Then all of a sudden I heard this growl, one I was all to familiar with. "One that gave me the chills."

"Danja," I yelled. Seconds later she exited the folds of the wooded area behind the park.

Her short black hair stood straight up on her back along with the tip of her clipped ears and tail, a sure sign that something was wrong.

She ran half way to me then turned and went back in the direction she had come from.

I gave Tanacia cynical look, put my cell phone in my back pocket and followed Danja.

She trotted about ten feet ahead not me and the deeper we went into the wooded area the heavier the smell of mold and rotting wood got.

The ground even got softer.

Tanacia jogged behind me.

"Taijae where in the hell are you going, I dont think this is a smart thing to do" I heard her say just as I caught up with Danja who stood over what appeared to be a body."

"The body of a female."

She wore a smoke gray DKNY blazer and a black pants suit with a Carolina Herrera hand bag that lay beside her untouched.

My first mind had me looking around that when I noticed a palm tree about seven feet away that was stained with blood.

 My second mind had me looking to see if I knew whom the women was but her face was to badly bashed in and he head was caked up with dirt and dried blood.

"What the fuck..!" I replied just above a whisper.

Tanacia had finally caught up with me. She walked up and put her hand on my shoulder and seen what I saw. For about thirty second there was complete silence before Tanacia said, "Oh shit that's Artencie Fulton."

I asked , "How can you tell?"

"Because that's what she wore to work yesterday and there was no way I could forget. I thought the outfit was rather tacky and how could I not remember those hideous Balenciaga sneakers plus she is the only one I know with a Coach Slim Easton watch with then pink Swarovski crystal like that one," replied Tanacia as she pointed in the direction of the females wrist.

I turned and looked at Tanacia who had a traumatizing look on her face, like she was going to pass out.

The three of us made our way back to the wooden picnic table at the park nearly out of breath.

Tanacia said, "This can't be happenings and who would want to kill Artencie Fulton and what was she doing out here in the first place," as the tears started to stream down her walnut colored skin.

I replied, "Hell if I know as I got my cell phone out of my pocket and dialed nine one one.

Part 2

Every time I closed my eyes and tried to focus all I could see was a battered face and body laying in the dirt and bloody leaves."

"After being at the precinct and interrogation room for hours Tanacia and I had failed brilliantly because neither one of us knew a thing and it was to early into the investigation to point fingers but it was clear that some one killed Ms. Fulton but who?

I knew just how the cities finest worked, my ex husband Edris was one of them. Undercover to be exact and you can't believe shit he said when it came to his work. Being decietful was his occupation which turned habitual.

After Tanacia and I gave our statements I contacted Edris and he didn't sound to happy.

His first words were, "How do you manage to keep getting caught up in these jams?"

"What do you mean, I'm not caught up in nothing."

He said, "Be foreal Ray and Stevie can clearly see that this Tanacia chick, your so called friend seems to have a complicated life and her problems are becoming yours."

"What is it that you want, details about Ms. Fulton. You never call then all of a sudden you ring me."

"Why didn't you call your new friend, I'm pretty sure you have him on speed dial."

I'd personally had enough of the bull shit and after Edris and I had seperated I knew deep in my heart that I would never marry again less alone give another man my heart.

Six months after the divorce was finalized I met a very handsome yet interesting young man named Avy Creighton who was a Search Engine Analyst for the F.B.I.

I had no complaints, he treated me like the queen that I truly was and had me head over hills but like all men he had his ways and solving mysteries and criminal justice was his life and come to think of it I might've emotionally disturbed him in some shape form or fashion because I hadn't heard from him in a few days.

I 'd called his cell and texted and he still hadn't return neither.

I asked Edris to tell me what what info they had gathered at the crime scene but he quickly shut me down .

His exact words were, "We're still gathering information and as of right now we have no lead what so ever."

I replied, "Come on with the bull shit, I know you know something now state the facts."

Dealing with Edris was worse than having the cramps and that's just what I told him applying pressure hoping that he would submit and give in.

Finally after five minutes of nagging and begging he finally nudged a bit, enough to shut them up.

He said, "Ms. Fulton was murdered what ever blunt object was used to kill her is no where near the site but we still have a lot of searching to do. And I know just how this is going to play out, they'll lable this an accident especially if that Daric Darnell ends up calling the shots.

Before he could finish his sentence I said, "How could you people be so ignorant, what about the blood on the tree?"

I couldn't believe what I was hearing and I sure as hell wasn't going for that fantastic fuck shit Daric Darnell was going to kick.

Before we hung up he said, "You didn't get this information from me and I better not hear a thing more outside of the conversation we've just had," an the line went dead.

The following morning at the office Danja sat stretched out next to

Mazzy. I quickly gathered the girls and gave them a brief rundown on all that had occurred and just like me they couldn't believe what they were hearing.

"I'll never forget, she was wearing tha beige looking pants suit, that hideous gray blazer and hand bag and those ugly ass Balenciaga sneakers," replied Tanacia.

Mazzy asked, "What business did she have in a dense wooded area like that and being that it was located near a plaza, none of this makes sense and I'll bet that somebody took her out there and fulfilled the intentions.

V'naevia added her ten cent's dousing her half a gallon of gas to the fire.

"Maybe she met someone at that plaza maybe had a few unpleasant words and they coaxed her into the wooded area bashing her face.

If I remember correct didn't you say you recall seeing blood on a tree close by where the body was found?"

I said, "Yes and they seem to be over looking what's evident!"

Kelley Renee' said, "Its amazing how they just sweeping this under the rug, people can get really retarded when its time to think logicly or maybe some one is already trying to cover this mess up."

Kelley Renee' was just beginning to weather the storm but she wasn't far from getting her feet wet. She was nineteen with a bright future ahead of her not to add outrageously intelligent and with out a shadow of a doubt one of a kind. She was currently attending Florida state university majoring in criminal justice, her dream is to be a lawyer. The crazy thing about her was that she wasn't into boys not one bit and that I couldn't understand because she was beautiful and fun to be around.

 Her dark skin was complimented by her hair which hung well past her shoulders.

I looked over at Tanacia who rattled the keys on the laptop as she typed away.

On this day she wore a pair of Old Navy jeans and an so here blue and gray halter topo with the matching finger nails and Foamposite tennis shoes.

Mazzy broke the silence she said, "I've actually talked to Ms Fulton weeks ago and she seemed to be a nice person."

Every body suddenly stopped what they were doing and looked in her direction.

Mazzy was always the same and she never

changed.

The gray highlight in her matched her eyes, the first person I'd met with eyes naturally that color which also seem to blend with what ever she wore.

I had to ask, "What was all that about?"

She said, "My grandson got into a little trouble with that fraternity over at Famu so I went to Daric Darnell, but I never got to speak with him,

Ms. Fulton just took my name and number and assured me that he would get back with me in due time."

"Did he ever contact you back?"

"Sure did and I can't complain about the services and he assured me that he would handle everything and that I had nothing to worry about," replied Mazzy.

I turned my attention to Tanacia who sat in silence with tears in her eye's.

Instantly the girls and I surrounded her assuring her that everything was going to be okay and she was going to be alright.

She said, "I can't believe that this is happening, even though Artencie and I had our differences I would never wish something so horrific to happen to her and we've got to find it who did this, you know Daric want be able to function with out her. She was the one who kept the firm in order. I wish I could take back all the bad things I said about her and even though she was a pain in the ass she didn't deserve to die. How can we prove that this wasn't an accident?"

I put my arms around her hugging her, only if she knew that Mr. Darnell was the reason that the cities finest is considering this to be an accident but what could I say when the man was regarded by society with the upmost respect and no one ever went against him. When he spoke the people listened, he was a peoples person.

"We've got to find out who killed Ms. Fulton, justice has to be served," replied Tanacia.

"Hold on a second, I'm all for that but for now we're going to leave it up the police. We don't know where to start and evenin if we wanted to help they wouldn't let us, you have to remember we are women."

Before I could finish my sentence Tanacia was out the door and Danja followed. She stopped momentarily looking back at me. My guardian angel had more sense than the average human.

Down at Darnell and Associates it felt very out of place. Every one looked sad and miserable but continued to work. Daric Darnell was a nicely built man, six' five in height, extremely handsome with a body to die for.

He wore Kkaki Michael Kors slacks and an olive green dress shirt that was a size to big hiding his well toned torso.

He spotted Tanacia and I wasted no time making his way to where we were. Tanacia sat down at her desk and instantly the phone started to ring. Daric in the either hand had the memory of an elephant because he knew just who I was.

He said, "Ms. Taijae Taylor sorry that we have to meet on such a sad notice."

I replied, "Any tragedy will bring people together."

He scanned me from head to toe with a flagrant look on his face and said, "We need more women like you in this world. Powerful, chocolate and just beautiful every square inch."

I was at a loss for words, this man was something else and a complete ass. All he did was kick big shit.

I watched as he bee lined through the office talking various before circling back around to where he took me the arm leading me into his office.

We walked into his office stoping behind the desk and said, "We need talk, and I promise justice will be served for Ms. Fulton and I'm really sorry that Ms. Thomas and yourself were the ones to discover such a tragedy. Ms. Fulton was hard working and indespensible.

Silence hung momentarily which was broken by the vibration of his cellphone inside of his desk.

He looked at the screen and said, "Pardon me!"

I sat patiently picking at the invisible dirt under my nails. My sixth sense told me that his finger prints were all on this and the conversation I had just heard didn't sound like a court case, it sounded more like a cold case.

He said, "Look the problem has been fixed it was just a simple misunderstanding and you don't have to worry about a thing because there want be a soul to testify and I will take the blame for going through with the operation but we'll talk more when we meet tonight."

He put the cell back in the desk and said, "Sorry about that, a concerned client with a twisted transcript but as I was saying we are working with the authorities on this because justice has to be served."

Every word he said went into one ear and out the other because I was more focused on the conversation that he'd just had. Something about this man didn't set right and at the very moment I couldn't put a finger on it.

Luckily I opted on driving my own vehicle to Tanacia's job because that's where I left her pressing buttons and answering phones.

As Danja and I rode the traffic I thought about the conversation that Daric Darnell had along with his actions which were more on the not concerned side of things and if he knew anything he didn't show it.

At this moment I needed to talk to Edris and like right now.

I dialed his number and on the second ring he answered sounding aggregated as ever.

He said, "What's going on Tai, unlike some one I know, people such as myself have to work for their living..."

Before he could finish singing his song I cut him off. I said, "Would you please just shut up, listen and stop your mess."

I gave him a briefing over what I'd just heard and how I really felt about Daric Darnell and it didn't surprise me not one bit that he was already a few steps ahead of me.

He said, "Were looking into all of this and were monitoring Daric's every move and don't be amazed if he ends up defending himself and I really hope your little friend has a good layer to go with that wardrobe, she's going to need it if this finger nail found on the scene is her's. We'll be picking her up before the week is out for questioning."

I was at a loss for words and couldn't believe what I was hearing and my heart felt like it was going to literally jump out of my chest. I knew my friend had problems but not these kind of problems.

I knew Tanacia like the back of my hand and she couldn't have committed a crime like this and contain her self with such innocence.

It just sounded insanely stupid and impossible.

Edris said, "We're all over this and I will try my best to get to the bottom of this, even if it includes sinking Mr Darnell's ship and I know that if we don't act on this now the shit might end up with the rest of the unsolved mysteries and with that being said there's statues when it comes to private practices so we couldn't bug the phones at the firm but that didn't stop us from linking with his cellphone.

We know that the guy that he's dealing with is Hatian and that they are suppose to meet tonight and this will determine rather or not he's he's clear on this go around or like I'm suspecting he's guilty.

I really hope your little friend isn't tied up in this mess and don't go spreading what we've discusssed remember this is an Investigation."

What I had just learned was secret safe with me but knowing that my friend could be a possible suspect in a murder was something else.

Before he hung up he said, "we'll talk later I have work to do."

Edris sat at the corner of Darnell Dr. watching the

five oversized computer screens that were customly built into the walls.

 On the screen he watched as a Black Audi SQ8 pulled into the parking space in front of the stone faced law firm.

Daric Darnell walked out of the building looked as of he was looking to see if he was begin watched then got in the vehicle.

Edris zoomed in in the plates tapping the mouse saving all of the data he'd just collected. Moments later the van came to life as it tailed the Audi Suv from a distance.

Fifteen minutes later Edris sat with his arms crossed over the two pistols that were located in his designer Burberry double shoulder holster.

Edris focused on Daric Darnell who stepped out of the SUV holding his cell phone to the side of his head and as he talked the expression on his face broadcasted pure anger. The conversation he was having wasn't a good one and by the time he'd tapped into the conversation all he heard was, "You got five minutes to get down here and you better have answers."

Daric got out of the SUV followed by a nicely dressed dread headed guy.

Daric flicked his wrist checking the time on his wrist watch. At this moment it was beyong the essence.

Meanwhile Edris and his crew waited and watch every soul that came and went from the resturant.

Being undercover was a dangerous job, he knew that all to well due to the fact that over the past five years the department had lost four detectives but Edris was determined to not become a statistic.

His partners Sharai Rose and Josiah Gancerez volunteered to go into the restaurant and get a visual on things.

Inside of the dimly lit eatery a middle aged hostess approached the table. She was beautiful with a million dollar smile but the dark rings around her eyes revealed the lack of sleep and a whole lot of fatigue.

The two struggled to hear soft voice over the

rhythm and blues as she asked to take their order.

She said, "What will you have to drink?

"Hienekin Zero,"replied Sharai who held up two fingers.

The waiter acknowledged the request and walked away. Minutes later she returned with their drinks. Josiah paid the tab and the waitress was on her way.

Three tables away Daric Darnell sat with the dread headed guy phone in hand.

Out of no where the dread head said, "Eliminate de problem mon before I do it for you, she witnessed everyting and I know if de right pressure is applied she will began to talk and at de moment mon I refuse to go out like you kind of people, you chose to play de game at your own risk now its time for you to put some points on de board and if anybody get in de way add them up too.

Edris listened and surveyed the people going into the eatery and noticed a young Haitian near the entrance smoking a cigarette. He took another drag of the cigarette then stepped on it with his shoe before entering the restaurant.

Ten minutes later the young Haitian exited the restaurant in a hurry.

Back inside of the van the two detectives confirmed that the Haitian had words with Daric Darnell and they weren't pleasant ones.

They then watched as the young man made his way to a maroon BMW M6. He got into the vehicle and sped out of the parking lot.

 Edris and his team followed.

After trailing him for five blocks the BMW came to a stop on South Jackson street, a street that was well known for drugs, guns and anything that was black market. People came from all over the world to buy and trade and still to this day no one knows who's really behind the operation and the streets stuck to the code because they never talked, no one wanted to end up dead in a ditch or food for the fish.

Edris and his team watched as a female walked to the passenger side of the car and got in. The dome light had been taken out because when she opened the door the interior remained dark.

At this moment Edris had no idea who the female was but he soon would find out. Minutes passed and things seemed normal until the darkness inside of the car was reversed by a brief flash of light.

The Haitian placed the barrel of the pistol to the side of the females temple firing once.

 The single round from the .40 caliber pistol pierced through the side of her head and Edris couldn't believe what he'd just seen. Detective Rose called in what they'd just seen but before authorities hit the scene the Haitian was long gone with the body.

Edris knew he wouldn't get far because at that very moment the tag was being ran.

 Apprehending Daric Darnell was next in the agenda and about to be charged with murder in the first and the recorded conversation that he had at the restaurant was evident enough. A few hours later Edris had Mr. Darnell in the interrogation room for questioning but he wasn't talking due to the fact that he knew the law better then they did and little did they know they were really going to have to bring their "A" game.

Dealing with a person who had friend's with higher power was going to be a task at hand.

Right before entering the interrogation room Edris learned that the maroon BMW with the dead female inside had been located, shockingly the female was also the owner of the vehicle but the question that remain was the where abouts of the driver.

In the interrogation room Edris questioned Daric Darnell about the conversation that he had at the restaurant with the shooter and just as he thought Daric Darnell denied any dealings but he quickly change his story after the recording were played back.

For a few moments he was at a loss for words as he'd been caught red handed in a lie and on his way to a holding cell but not for long because his money and power was surely going to bail him out.

The few hours that sat in that holding cell was definitley his last and before they knew it he was bailed out on a million dollar bond.

Edris knew that in order to bring this man down they were going to really need the people on their side.

Before Edris left the precinct he read over the report and come to find out the female was one of Daric Darnell's puppets. This was just the beginning and a long way from the end as the bodies would soon start to pile up.

Back at his apartment Edris stared out the window at the stars as he and Taijae put two and two together and just as she had suspected in the begining Daric Darnell had ties in some fishy business now all she hoped that Tanacia didn't have any association with the murder of her co-worker.

After discovering that the female that was killed in the car side work for Darnell the next question was what kind of side work did she do, was that fingernail that was found on the scene hers?

As of now there were no matches due to the fact that they were synthetic along with the weather condition's which altered any evidence that was once there.

Edris made a quick dinner and we tried our best to set our differences aside and act civilized but that alone wasn't an easy task.

 The man I thought i'd spend the rest of my life with and love for an enternity was double dealing.

He charmed his way into my life and like a fool I

feel face forward for him but those days were now long gone.

Time seemed to fly as we made contradictions and conclusions about what had taken place earlier and I was determined to get to the bottom of this myself.

****

An hour later I was back at my place and time was winding down for Tanacia and I to meet. I changed into all black attire and called Danja.

I said, "Come on girl let's go see our girl and break off into Daric Darnell's office, theres more evidence in there and Tanacia knows just where it's all stashed, even you know our girl would never commit any crime and I'm going to prove that Daric Darnell is connected to more than they think."

She looked at me, head turned side ways like she clearly understood every word I'd said.

It wasn't long before Tanacia and I arrived at Daric Darnell's office. The parking space behind the building was vacant and the sound of the doors slamming echoed all around. Tanacia and I approached the rear entrance looking through doubled glass window.

On the inside it was pitch black, meaning you couldn't see a thing but that didn't mean there wasn't some one in there.

My sixth sense kicked in and I began to remember how the office was layed out.

I told Tanacia to hold on as I walked to the dark corner looking up at the window to Daric Darnell's office.

She looked to her left and right nervously and said, "You are not leaving me here alone!"

"I said you want be alone because Danja will be here with you."

I turned to her and said, "Protection girl!"

Danja stood up and moved into position next to Tanacia.

As I walked away Tanacia said, "Don't take all day, this feeling that I have tell's me that something isn't right.

By time she'd finished complaining I was on my way back to her ready to go in this building.

I hadn't realized how scary my friend really was until she got ready to put in the pass code to the office.

She shook like a palm tree off the the ocean breeze and mumbled to her self, "This is all an illusion."

Once we were on the inside of the office we made our way into his office and I instantly locked in on the filing cabinet in the corner before slipping back behind the wall.

I know I seen a shadow and Danja did too as she instantly went into guard mode.

Lowly she growled and I knew at that moment I wasn't tripping.

This wasn't an illusion or dream.

Danja looked back at me then raced to a door located behind Daric Darnell's desk where she paced back and forth sniffing.

Not thinking I went for the door because we weren't suppose to be there and who ever else was in there wasn't either.

Tanacia said, "That might not be a good idea," but before she could finish her sentence I said, "Tanacia something or some one is in there."

From the outside looking in the place looked vacant.

In a low tone Tanacia said, "I really don't think this is a good idea after all, we are breaking and entering."

I said, "This ain't shit compared to what's about to happen if that finger nail found on the scene cone back a match."

"I just want to go home," she whispered.

"We will but first let's see what's really going on behind this door."

I turned my attention to Danja who paced back and forth in front of the door.

Danja had gained a sixth sense and if some one was mad, upset, in danger or not feeling well some how or another she could detect.

Even if the person had left hours before.

I turned to her and said, " Is there some one behind that door girl."

She growled lowly as she pointing her nose under towards the door.

I said, "Tanacia do you have access to that door."

She looked at me with fear all over her face and said, "Let's just leave and I hope your not planning on going in there."

I looked over at her and just as I was about to speak there was a loud thump on the other side of the door alerting Danja.

She said, Did you hear that."

I looked at her, she looked at Danja and Danja was trying to get under that door.

I told her to move from in front of the door just in case some one came out swinging or shooting,

I didn't want her to get caught in the line of fire but I just knew it was a rat making the ruckus.

Tanacia peeked around the wall pressing her body as close as she could from the door way of Mr. Darnell's office and said, "Can Danja smell through doors.

 I heard her every word but I didn't say a thing as I opened the door side stepping out out of view.

It swung open and Danja
bolted in the room.

I listened as she moved
around before I peered
in feeling the wall for the
light switch.

I knew it wasn't a good
idea to turn on the light
but I just had to see.
Momentarily I hit the
switch and Danja stood
in the middle of the room
looking at the window.

I knew by her actions
that no one was in the
room at the moment but
some one had been

there.

I hadn't realized that I failed to breathe as the moment had intensified.

Tanacia walked in behind me and pointed at the filing cabinets in the back of the room before turning the light off.

I said, "What are you doing, I need to see!"

"Yeah and somebody will see the light and know that we are here."

She was right.

I pulled out my phone and used the light on it.

Outside the window I thought I'd seen a flash of light which were the motion sensored lights that were on the building.

I walked over to the window peeking out at the dark area where I know for a fact I saw something move.

This was no illusion.

I watched for a few minutes but nothing happened.

Tanacia thumbed through the files which she knew were in order because Artencie had her own way of doing things. She coded her files with colored tabs.

Tanacia continued to thumb through the files and said, "Look at this, she has filing section that say 'Tax Write Offs and Personal compensation.'"

I squatted down next looking at the purple tabs on the folders which all contained cream colored envelopes with computer printed label.

"See this the shit I'm talking about, this bitch has a file with my name on it then look there's more than one ," replied Tanacia.

I looked at Tanacia and said, "Maybe you are right, she did have it out for you!"

Out of no where Danja let off a bark that echoed through the empty building, I quickly turned off the light on my cellphone.

I said, "Tanacia go and make sure the door we entered is secured but she didn't move. She was stuck in that one spot.

I had to literally push her to get her to moving and just as I did the the door burst open and Danja went into a frenzy.

The illusion that I saw was of a man wearing a ski mask armed with a pistol.

I screamed for Danja just as the man pointed the gun in my direction and out of no where she flung herself against his leg causing him fall.

He took a few unsuccessful swings at Danja which only made things worse as she twisted and turned tightning her grip, she was taught to not let go and would hold until I told her otherwise then some how or another Danja must have lightened up on her grip because the man suddenly broke free.

He twisted around, looked at me then the direction of the door before taking off.

Danja let off a deep growl and shot out behind the masked man into the darkness.

 I called her name but she ignored me.

In what I concluded as the break room, Tanacia sat in the corner balled up with her hands over her ears. I took a quick look around then ran back to the door.

Danja stood just a few feet away looking up the side of the building as if the man had scaled to the roof.

Tanacia stood close by and Danja sensed me as she turned heading in my direction.

Her head hung low because knew who ever the masked man was had gotten away, we had really fucked up all the way around the board.

I knelt down massaged her entire body in search of a flinch but she seemed fine.

Suddenly I had this very awful feeling, the feeling that you felt when you were being watched.

I looked left and right but there was not a soul in sight.

I said under my breath, "Where did he go Danja?"

Danja ran back to the same spot where she had been moments before looking up the wall.

I thought to myself what better way to lose a dog than to scale a wall as I then noticed the fire escape.

We all walked to down the dimly lit side street from one end to another but at three in the morning there wasn't a soul to be recon with.

While we were out looking I guess the masked man circled back around and re-entered the the office.

In a matter of minutes the same files that we were just looking through were scattered all over the room.

I'd never seen so much destruction done in silence.

I made sure we weren't leaving any evidence and by now the masked man was long gone at least that's what we were hoping.

It all just seemed and felt weird.

The files were scattered out and it was really hard to tell rather any were missing.

As I began to gather the papers Tanacia looked around the room then up at the camera's that were located in every other corner.

She said, "We might be in trouble I totally forgot about the surveillance camera's through out this motherfucker."

It took me a few minutes before I realized that the files on Tanacia, the tax write off and personal compensation were gone.

Twenty minutes later we had the files back in place and ready to leave. In actuality we were in a lot of trouble if Daric Darnell went back on the camera's.

The three of us jogged across the vacant parking lot and about ten feet from the car Danja stopped and turned back in the direction of the law firm as if some one had called her, she knew something wasn't right.

Tanacia said "Do you think we need to call the police?"

I said, "Not unless you want to sit in the county jail but before I could finish my sentence out of no where Tanacia's head split in half, her body dropped to the knee's falling face forward on the pavement as the blood ran continues like a faucet. Danja went into a frenzy and I did too.

Tanacia had been murdered in cold blood right in front of me and I had no clue as to who the shooter was.

 I had lost a dear friend but how was I going to explain this to Edris, I thought as I dialed nine one one.

 I was in this shit up to my neck now and Edris warned me but I wouldn't listen.

La'mar Donald

I knew for a fact Daric Darnell had something to hide and something up his sleeves and before I went down I was going to make sure he went first.

Hey family and friends if you made it this far then i know you enjoyed yet another one of my twisted tales and make sure to stay tuned for pt. 2 and find out who's really responsible for these mishaps.

Author La'mar Donald

Follow Me:

FB@Author La'mar Donald

Web page:

Author La'mar Donald.Webador.com

Cover Design:

Element of Design by CHOPPTRIGG